Jam Session

Barry Bonds

Terri Dougherty
ABDO Publishing Company

visit us at
www.abdopub.com

Published by ABDO & Daughters, an imprint of ABDO Publishing Company, 4940 Viking Drive, Suite 622, Edina, Minnesota 55435. Copyright © 2002 by Abdo Consulting Group, Inc. International copyrights reserved in all countries. No part of this book may be reproduced in any form without written permission from the publisher.

Printed in the United States.

Cover and Interior Photo credits: All-Sport, AP/Wide World, Corbis

Edited by Paul Joseph

Library of Congress Cataloging-in-Publication Data

Dougherty, Terri.
    Barry Bonds / Terri Dougherty.
    p. cm. — (Jam session)
    Includes index.
    Summary: Presents a biography of the power hitter for the San Francisco Giants who broke Mark McGwire's single-season home run record in 2001.
    ISBN 1-57765-675-X
    1. Bonds, Barry, 1964—Juvenile literature. 2. Baseball players—United States—Biography—Juvenile literature. [1. Bonds, Barry 1964- 2. Baseball players. 3. African Americans—Biography.] I. Title. II. Series.

    GV865.B637 D68 2002
    796.357'092—dc21
    [B]
                                                           2001055276

Contents

A Giant Among Sluggers

*B*arry Bonds was concentrating on the fastball rushing toward him from Los Angeles Dodgers pitcher Chan Ho Park. It was just what he wanted to see. The San Francisco Giants slugger extended his arms, flicked his wrists, and rocketed the ball over the right-center field fence and into baseball history.

Barry's 71st home run of the season on October 5, 2001, set a record for home runs in a season. He raised his arm in the air and pointed skyward as he circled the bases at Pacific Bell Park in San Francisco.

After crossing home plate he lifted his son, Nikolai, a Giants batboy, into the air. His teammates surrounded him. The number 71 flashed on the scoreboard and fireworks popped as he hugged family members. After the game he was honored in a ceremony that included his godfather, Hall-of-Famer Willie Mays. "You couldn't even dream about putting together a season like this," Bonds said.

Mark McGwire, who had set the previous home run record at 70 in 1998, was impressed by Barry's ability. "What he's done, it's absolutely phenomenal," McGwire said. "It's in the stratosphere."

Barry is a four-time National League Most Valuable Player (MVP). He has used power at the plate, skill in the field, and cunning base running to become one of the greatest baseball players of all time.

The home run record was especially rewarding because pitchers were reluctant to throw strikes to Barry. Pitchers often thought it better to walk the 230-pound left-handed slugger than to risk the ball ending up out of the stadium.

"It's hard to just keep taking pitches all the time," Barry said. "You don't get any opportunities. You feel like you're losing your swing."

Barry, however, stayed focused and added two more home runs to put the new record at 73. But the homers were only part of what some baseball historians called the greatest season ever by a major-league player.

By walking 177 times, Barry broke Babe Ruth's 78-year-old record for walks in a season. His slugging percentage of .863 topped Ruth's old mark, set in 1920. Barry's powerful ability at the plate was further evidenced by a .515 on-base percentage, the highest in the National League since John McGraw's .547 in 1899.

"I think this is awesome," Giants manager Dusty Baker said. "This was one of the greatest years— no, it was *the* greatest year— I have seen from a single person."

Barry rounds the bases after hitting home run #73.

Baseball Bonds Family Together

*B*aseball has always been a part of Barry's life. His father, Bobby, signed with the Giants soon after Barry was born on July 24, 1964, in Riverside, California.

There were other sports stars in his family, too. An uncle played college football and an aunt, Rosie, won the 80-meter low hurdles in the U.S. Olympic trials and competed in the 1964 Olympics.

When Barry was very young his dad played for several minor-league teams. It was often too expensive for Barry and his mom to live with his dad while he was playing in the minors. They lived in California while Bobby played ball.

Barry soon showed that he had inherited his father's baseball talent. As a two-year-old he comfortably swung his plastic bat so hard that he broke a window with a wiffle ball. When his father moved up to the major leagues in 1968, Barry was right there with him, warming up with the players before the game. Wearing a little Giants uniform, he shagged fly balls in the Candlestick Park outfield with his dad and Mays. "I was too young to bat with them," Barry said. "But I could compete with them in the field."

Barry and his son Nikolai.

Barry and his brothers would take bubble gum from the clubhouse and hit balls in batting practice before the players arrived. Barry wanted to be just like his dad and the other ballplayers. "Barry has a lot of Bobby in him, as far as baseball goes," said his mom, Pat. "Barry has goals, and that was Bobby, too."

Bobby Bonds was known for stealing bases and hitting home runs. However, he was often criticized for striking out often, and was traded frequently. He played for eight teams in his 14-year major-league career.

Bobby's traveling was hard on Barry, who usually stayed in California with his mother, grandmother, and brothers.

However, when Barry got to go to the ballpark he met and learned from superstars such as Nolan Ryan, Catfish Hunter, and Thurman Munson. Mays gave him advice about stopping teams by playing well in the outfield, and he learned defense from others as well.

On bat day, Barry would get a free bat at the ballpark. The big bats helped him hone his quick-swinging style. "The free bats we got were heavy," Barry said. "I had to choke up. It became a habit."

By the time he was 10, Barry was a top player in Little League. His father was often absent from Barry's games because of his job. When he could make it he often stayed in the background so he wouldn't get attention from the crowd.

Barry may not have known that his dad was watching, but by the time Barry was in ninth grade his father knew that his son had a special gift for baseball.

Barry and his father Bobby.

A Major Leap to Big Leagues

*B*arry played baseball, basketball, and football at Serra High School in San Mateo, California. He was such a talented baseball player that the Giants offered him a $75,000 contract when he graduated in 1982.

Barry wasn't certain that he wanted to play professional baseball right after high school, however. He was also considering going to college. His father advised him to ask for $5,000 more. When Barry didn't get it, he decided to play baseball at Arizona State University.

In college, Barry was named to the all-Pac 10 Conference team three years in a row and to *The Sporting News* all-America team in 1985. As a junior he hit 23 home runs and had a .368 batting average. He got along well with his coach, but was indifferent toward his teammates.

"I never saw a teammate care about him," said his coach, Jim Brock. "Part of it would be his being rude, inconsiderate, and self-centered. He bragged about the money he turned down, and he popped off about his dad. I don't think he ever figured out what to do to get people to like him."

Barry left Arizona State after his junior year, when the Pittsburgh Pirates made him the sixth pick in the first round of the 1985 free-agent draft. After playing only 115 games in the minor leagues he was called up to the majors at age 21.

Expectations were high when Barry joined the Pirates. His father had spent his career trying to live up to comparisons with Mays, and Barry began his by being compared to his father. Anything less than greatness for Barry would be considered failure.

Dr. Kathy Dodd

Mr. Pleas Thompson

Judge Caroline Wall

The ExPress Newspaper April

Bonds Cashes In

*L*ess than a year after he had been chosen in the free-agent draft, Barry was the starting center fielder and leadoff hitter with the Pirates. He quickly showed that he belonged. He hit a double on his second day with the team, and in less than a week he hit his first home run. In 1986, he led National League rookies in home runs, runs batted in, stolen bases, and walks.

The 6-foot-2, 185-pounder switched from center field to left field on May 30, 1987. In his first three full seasons with the Pirates he averaged 23 home runs, 27 stolen bases, and a .264 batting average. Barry was doing all right, but there was the feeling that he could do better.

"Barry's the only individual I've met who can turn it on and turn it off. I didn't think that could be done," Pittsburgh outfielder R.J. Reynolds said. "I think one day he will put up numbers no one can believe."

Criticism of his father had stung Barry when he was a child. Although Bobby hit 30 home runs and stole 30 bases in a season five times, three more than Mays, he still fell short of some people's expectations. Barry used his dad's experiences to come to terms with what other people thought of him.

"No one gives my dad credit for what he did, and they want to put me in the same category," Barry said. "He did 30-30 five times, and they say he never became the ballplayer he should have become. So I don't care whether they like me or they don't like me."

Whether he cared about his popularity or not, Barry's performance improved on the field. He was moved to the heart of the batting order, and in 1990 his average improved to .301. "I wasn't comfortable leading off," Barry said. "Before coming to the big leagues, I was never a leadoff hitter, in Little League or at any point. I was frustrated because I was in a lot of situations with two outs. I just felt I could do more, and I think I pressed in the leadoff spot to prove that I could do more."

That season he put up spectacular numbers and earned his first MVP and Gold Glove awards. He hit 33 home runs, stole 52 bases, drove in 114 runs, and scored 104 runs. "I like driving in runs. I like being in situations where the pitcher has to be at his best," Barry said. "That's when I figure that I'm at my best. When you have runners on first and second, the pitcher has to bear down and make his best pitch. That makes me want to bear down and be a better hitter."

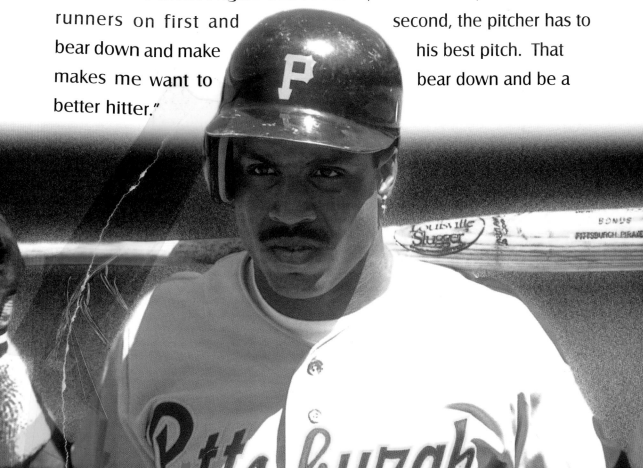

Barry made his first postseason appearance that year after the Pirates won the National League East. However, Barry struggled as the Pirates lost to the Cincinnati Reds, four games to two, in the NL championship series.

Barry continued to play well during the regular season, coming in second in the MVP voting in 1991 and winning his second MVP award in 1992. However, the Pirates couldn't get past the Atlanta Braves in the '91 and '92 league championship series. Barry only had a .191 average, one home run, and three RBI in his three postseason appearances.

Although he was a great player, his aloof attitude made him unpopular in Pittsburgh and he was criticized for his arrogance. He once walked around a circle of his teammates, who were stretching, tapping them on the shoulder or cap. He said, "On my birthday, I just wanted to give you all a gift. A little bit of my talent."

Barry defended his demeanor, saying he was just concentrating on doing his job. He used his brash attitude to motivate himself on the field. "Since I was a kid, I've had a stamp on my neck: Barry Bonds has a bad attitude and only thinks of himself," he said. "Who else am I supposed to think about out there? I go out there to put up the best numbers to help us win. That's being part of the team."

Barry was a superstar Pittsburgh couldn't afford to keep when he became a free agent after the 1992 season. He took a $43 million offer from the Giants and became the highest-paid player in baseball at that time. The deal was sweetened when his father became the Giants hitting coach. Father and son were going home.

"This year has been exceptionally good. It's nice to go places and the whole city is rooting for you."

He's Barry, Barry Good

The Giants gave Barry what he wanted. In addition to the high salary, he got his own hotel suite on the road. In the clubhouse, he relaxed in a recliner and watched a big screen TV. Because of this, Barry was under pressure to produce. In 1993, he showed he could do it, hitting a homer in his first at-bat for the Giants and winning his third MVP award that season. Playing left field and wearing 25, his dad's old number, Barry helped the Giants improve their number of wins from 72 to 103.

Under the watchful eye of his father, he batted .336 with 46 home runs and 123 RBI. His father didn't let Barry get complacent about his swing. "When Barry does something I don't like, I tell him," Bobby said. "I'm not the type to look the other way. I don't care how much money he makes, he's still my son. I think I'm harder on Barry than I am on other players."

Although Barry's attitude didn't always win people over, teammates respected his ability at the plate, his home runs, his base stealing, and stunning catches in the outfield. "He can play," Mays observed. "They're not paying him for any other reason."

Barry continued to hit home runs and steal bases over the next several seasons. In 1996, he became a member of the elite 300 home run, 300 stolen base club. He set an NL record with 151 walks, and was the second player in history to hit 40 home runs and steal 40 bases in a season.

"The best thing that happened to me was going home. The press and fans in my hometown are very good about me and what I do," he said. "They really like me. That's a big difference. When they say there's no place like home, there's no place like home."

Barry had 40 home runs and 101 RBI the next season, which he capped with a strong finish to help the Giants win the NL West division over the Dodgers. In 1998, he became the first player in major-league history to hit 400 home runs and steal 400 bases.

Barry felt like he was coming into the prime of his career. In 2000, he set career highs in home runs and slugging percentage and tied his career best for runs scored.

Barry Gets Bigger and Better

The three-time MVP never rested on his accomplishments. He continued to work, lifting weights to improve his strength. By 2001, he had bulked up to 228 pounds, weighing about 40 pounds more than he did when he came into the league. "I've always wanted to be known as a complete player," he said.

Barry still lacked a stellar postseason highlight, but that didn't take away from his ability. "Anyone who judges Barry on how he's hit in the postseason is crazy," Baker said. "He's one of the all-time greats, period."

Barry had hit a career-high 49 home runs in 2000 but even he couldn't have guessed what he would do in 2001.

By mid-August he had hit the most home runs of any Giant in a season. He broke Mays' record of 52 with a 420-foot three-run blast that went into the right-field bleachers at Pacific Bell Park. He didn't want to think about setting a major-league record, however.

"Right now, I'm just thinking about winning," he said. "I don't need it (the record). I need to win."

As the season neared its close, Barry continued to pound the ball. He never went into a slump. In September, he didn't go more than two games without hitting a home run and was thankful to have the stamina to keep going.

"I'm healthy. I feel better at 37 than I did at 36 or 35," he said. "I'm playing like a kid more than I ever did before. That's why I feel the blessing inside of me, because no 37-year-old man is supposed to be running around the field like I do. I can do it for the next five years, six years. Why not?"

The season's closing weeks were marred by tragic terrorist attacks in New York City and Washington, D.C. Baseball games were suspended as the nation mourned. When games resumed, Barry quietly continued to hit home runs.

Personal tragedy struck the superstar with less than two weeks to go in the season when a close friend died unexpectedly. Barry grieved, and hit a home run in his friend's honor. Although tragic events swirled around him off the field, Barry never lost his focus at the plate.

"It's not that easy to hit home runs, and it's like he's playing in a Little League park now," San Diego Padres manager Bruce Bochy said after Barry hit his 69th home run of the year, which landed in San Francisco Bay. "He's just a wrecking crew. There's no way to get him out."

As the pressure intensified, Barry's father and godfather offered him advice. " 'Stay patient. Stay patient'," Barry said they told him. "The main job is winning. The best thing they told me is that if I keep doing my job, eventually it has to come."

Barry's teammates rallied around him as he neared the record. "He just continues to impress," teammate Jeff Kent said. "We've watched him in amazement all year long."

When he tied McGwire's record of 70 on October 4, his teammates ran from the dugout to congratulate him after he rounded the bases with his arms raised. "I just got a good pitch to hit," Bonds said.

He ended the season with his 73rd home run, sending a knuckleball from Dodgers pitcher Dennis Springer over the right-field wall. He was just as pleased that the Giants won the game. "This was a great, great way to end it, with a victory and a home run," he said. "You can't ask for anything better. I never thought I could do it."

Barry became a free agent at the end of the 2001 season and didn't know if he would continue to play with the Giants. But he was satisfied with how things had gone for him in San Francisco.

"This is my home," he said. "It has been my home since 1968 when my dad came here. This will always be my home. My relationship has been up and down, but for the most part it has been good. This year has been exceptionally good."

No matter where Barry Bonds plays he will continue to amaze fans and players alike. And when his career ends he will most certainly be remembered as one of the greatest hitters the game has ever seen.

Barry Bonds tips his cap to the San Francisco fans after hitting his 72nd home run.

Barry Bonds' Batting Statistics

Year	Team	Level	Avg.	HR	RBI	SB
1985	Prince William (Va.)	Class A	.299	13	37	15
1986	Hawaii	Class AAA	.311	7	37	16
	Pittsburgh	Majors	.223	16	48	36
1987	Pittsburgh	Majors	.261	25	59	32
1988	Pittsburgh	Majors	.283	24	58	17
1989	Pittsburgh	Majors	.248	19	58	32
1990	Pittsburgh	Majors	.301	33	114	52
1991	Pittsburgh	Majors	.292	25	116	43
1992	Pittsburgh	Majors	.311	34	103	39
1993	San Francisco	Majors	.336	46	123	29
1994	San Francisco	Majors	.312	37	81	29
1995	San Francisco	Majors	.294	33	104	31
1996	San Francisco	Majors	.308	42	129	40
1997	San Francisco	Majors	.291	40	101	37
1998	San Francisco	Majors	.303	37	122	28
1999	San Francisco	Majors	.262	34	83	15
2000	San Francisco	Majors	.306	49	106	11
2001	San Francisco	Majors	.328	73	137	13
Totals			.292	567	1,542	484

Barry Bonds' NL Division Series Batting Statistics

Year	Team	Opponent	Avg.	HR	RBI	SB
1997	San Francisco	Florida	.250	0	2	1
2000	San Francisco	New York Mets	.176	0	1	1

Barry Bonds' NL Championship Series Batting Statistics

Year	Team	Opponent	Avg.	HR	RBI	SB
1990	Pittsburgh	Cincinnati	.167	0	1	2
1991	Pittsburgh	Atlanta	.148	0	0	3
1992	Pittsburgh	Atlanta	.261	1	2	1

KEY: Avg. - Batting average; HR - Home runs; RBI - Runs batted in; SB - Stolen bases.

Barry Lamar Bonds Profile

Born: July 24, 1964, in Riverside, California

Height: 6-foot-2

Weight: 228 pounds

Position: Left fielder

Bats: Left

Throws: Left

Resides: Los Altos Hills, California

Family: Wife, Liz; son, Nikolai;
daughters, Shikari and Aisha; Dad, Bobby;
Mom, Patricia; Brothers, Ricky and Bobby, Jr.

Personal: Former Giants star and hitting coach Bobby Bonds is his father ... Barry and his father hold the all-time father-son records for HR, RBI, and stolen bases ... Barry and Bobby are the only players in major-league history to have 30 HRs and 30 stolen bases in a season five times ... Barry's godfather is Hall-of-Famer and former Giants great Willie Mays ... Barry's aunt, Rosie Bonds, once held U.S. women's record in 80-meter hurdles and was on '64 U.S. Olympic team ... graduated from Serra (San Mateo, California) High School in 1982 ... Starred in baseball, football, and basketball at Serra ... Hit .404 over three varsity seasons, including .467 as prep all-American his senior year ... Played three seasons for Arizona State University, hitting .347 for his career with 45 homers and 175 RBI ... tied NCAA record with seven consecutive hits in College World Series as a sophomore ... Was named to all-time CWS team in 1996 ... Hobbies include weightlifting, martial arts, and dancing ... 10-handicap golfer ... Under auspices of Barry Bonds Family Foundation, spearheaded bone marrow campaign that raised considerable funds for families whose loved ones have leukemia or related blood disorders ... Has been involved in many other community projects ... Has appeared in movies and on television.

Awards and Honors

★ Named 1990s Player of the Decade by *The Sporting News.*

★ Won four NL Most Valuable Player awards (1990, '92, '93, 2001).

★ Named to 10 all-star teams.

★ Won nine Gold Gloves.

★ Only player in major-league history with 400 HRs and 400 stolen bases.

★ Only NL player to hit 40 homers and steal 40 bases in a season ('96).

Barry receiving one of his
nine Gold Glove awards.

Chronology

July 24, 1964 - Barry Lamar Bonds is born in Riverside, California.

1982 - Graduates from Serra High School in San Mateo, California. Drafted in second round by Giants, but elects to attend Arizona State University, where he plays for three seasons.

1985 - Begins pro career at Prince William (Virginia) of Class A Carolina League after being drafted with the sixth pick of the first round by Pittsburgh.

1986 - Plays 44 games for Class AAA Hawaii before contract is purchased by Pirates on May 30. Leads NL rookies in homers, RBI, stolen bases, and walks.

1987 - Opens season in center field, but switches to left field on May 30.

1990 - Wins NL MVP award and Major League Player of Year award from *The Sporting News*. Named to NL all-star team for first time.

1991 - Is second to Atlanta's Terry Pendleton in MVP voting.

1992 - Wins second MVP award. As free agent, signs contract with Giants on December 8.

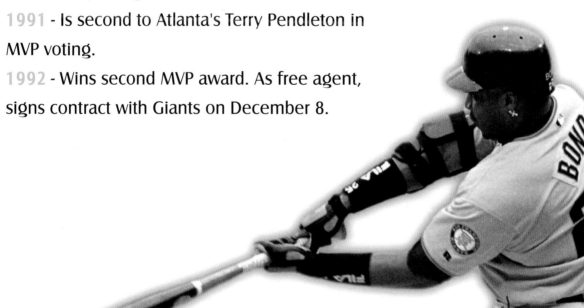

1993 - Named The Associated Press Major League Player of Year. Wins S. Rae Hickok award as nation's top professional athlete. Wins third NL MVP award. Leads NL in homers (46), RBI (123), slugging percentage (.677), and on-base percentage (.458), and is second in runs (129) and fourth in hitting (.336). Leading vote-getter in fan balloting for All-Star Game.

1994 - Is on pace for 52 homers and 114 RBI before players' strike wipes out final seven weeks of season.

1995 - Leading NL vote-getter for All-Star Game.

1996 - Becomes only NL player to hit 40 homers and steal 40 bases in a season.

1997 - Hits two inside-the-park homers.

1998 - Hits career-high 44 doubles. Hits 451-foot homer in All-Star Game.

1999 - Several injuries limit him to 102 games. Gets 2,000th career hit.

2000 - Finishes second in MVP voting to teammate Jeff Kent. Hits career-high 49 homers.

2001 - Wins fourth NL MVP award. Sets single-season major-league records for home runs (73), slugging percentage (.863), and walks (177). Breaks professional baseball single-season record of 72 home runs, set by Joe Bauman in Class C Longhorn League in 1954.

60-homer seasons in major-league history

Name	Year	Team	HR
Barry Bonds	2001	San Francisco	73
Mark McGwire	1998	St. Louis	70
Sammy Sosa	1998	Chicago Cubs	66
Mark McGwire	1999	St. Louis	65
Sammy Sosa	2001	Chicago Cubs	64
Sammy Sosa	1999	Chicago Cubs	63
Roger Maris	1961	N.Y. Yankees	61
Babe Ruth	1927	N.Y. Yankees	60

Top 10 all-time major-league home run leaders

Name	First Year	Last year	Total HR
Hank Aaron	1954	1976	755
Babe Ruth	1914	1935	714
Willie Mays	1951	1973	660
Frank Robinson	1956	1976	586
Mark McGwire	1986	2001	583
Harmon Killebrew	1954	1975	573
Barry Bonds	1986		567
Reggie Jackson	1967	1987	563
Mike Schmidt	1972	1989	548
Mickey Mantle	1951	1968	536

Home run leaders Barry Bonds and Sammy Sosa talk before an All Star game.

Glossary

CENTER FIELDER – The player in the middle part of the outfield.

DRAFT – A system that gives baseball teams a chance to choose new players.

FASTBALL – A pitch thrown at full speed.

FREE AGENT – A player who can sign with any team.

HOME RUN – A hit that allows the batter to reach home plate safely. Almost always, the ball is hit out of the field of play.

LEADOFF HITTER – The first hitter in the batting order.

MINOR LEAGUE – A group of professional teams in a league below the major leagues.

MVP – Most Valuable Player.

NL – National League, one of the two organizations (along with the American League) that make up Major League Baseball, the highest level of professional baseball. The AL and NL are also called the "big leagues" or "major leagues."

RBI – Run batted in. A player gets an RBI when he drives in a run.

SLUGGING PERCENTAGE – A player's total bases divided by the number of at-bats.

STEAL – To run to the next base without the ball being hit.

STRIKE OUT – To make an out in baseball with three strikes.

WALK – To reach first base after a pitcher throws four balls.

Index